The Journey of Curious Philip Ajere LaBier

A Storybook Inspired by the Noble Eightfold Path

By Philip K.Abbott

Forward By His Eminence Doctor Yon Seng Yeath

Volume One | English Edition

eBook ISBN: 979-8-89795-971-6
Paperback ISBN: 979-8-89795-972-3
Hardcover ISBN: 979-8-89795-973-0

www.penguinpublishers.org

This edition has been developed in partnership with Preah Sihanouk Raja Buddhist University and Buddhism for Education of Cambodia (BEC), as part of an international peace education initiative.

Author's Acknowledgments

The genesis of this journey lies in the doctoral research I conducted in post-genocide Cambodia with socially engaged Theravāda Buddhist monks at Buddhism for Education of Cambodia (BEC).

What began as an academic inquiry about how Buddhist monks understand and practice conflict analysis and resolution evolved into a life-transforming experience, rooted in shared learning, humility, and heartfelt collaboration.

I am grateful to the monks of BEC, especially Venerable Hak Sienghai, whose wisdom, generosity, and unwavering compassion illuminated the path forward.

Rather than conducting research *on* or *about* these virtuous individuals in the traditional sense, I was privileged to walk *with* them in a spirit of participatory action research—living among them, learning together, and exploring how peace, happiness, and social harmony can be cultivated from within.

Their daily embodiment of the Noble Eightfold Path offered profound teachings and living examples of inner transformation. Their commitment to peace training and peace praxis continues to inspire and guide those seeking a gentler, kinder, and more generous world. This storybook is lovingly dedicated to these monks.

I offer my highest praise and admiration to Odom Vansivon, a Cambodian woman, who, despite having only a fifth-grade education, introduced me to the Noble Eightfold Path during my first visit to Cambodia. Walking

alongside Venerable Maha Ghosananda in the Dhammayietra peace walk, she embodied compassion and peace, reflecting the wise influence women have had in shaping both my life and my spiritual journey.

I also honor the resilient Cambodian people, especially individuals like Uy Sithorn, whose courage and dignity in the face of deep suffering remind us that even amid hardship, compassion and hope can take root and blossom. Their warmth, openness, and generosity touched me deeply and shaped the heart of this work.

I extend sincere thanks to the faculty at George Mason University, particularly Dr. Susan Allen and the Action Research Working Group, for nurturing a research approach grounded in reflection, ethical inquiry, and mutual transformation.

Special thanks to the talented graphic design team at Preah Sihanouk Raja Buddhist University in Phnom Penh—Venerable Thai Raksmey, Noy Samart, and Keo Vichith—for their outstanding contributions. Their enthusiasm and creative spirit not only enhanced the visual storytelling of this short story but also embodied the essence of the participatory action research approach from which it was born.

Finally, to my beloved wife, Maya—thank you for your patience, your steadfast love, and your courageous heart. Your presence made every step of this journey more meaningful.

The Kingdom of Cambodia

Table of Contents

List of Illustrations

✦

Preface

This story began with a big question I had carried in my heart and mind for a long time:

"Who am I… really?"

I had spent many years as an American soldier and diplomat, traveling the world, wearing a military uniform with medals, and making important decisions. But even with all that, I still felt like something was missing. Deep inside, I didn't feel truly peaceful.

Something seemed to cloud my heart and mind—an unease that no success could erase.

Then, one day, I traveled to a faraway land called the Kingdom of Cambodia, a place full of golden temples, gentle smiles, and wise Buddhist monks.

These monks were not as angry or strict as I often experienced living and working as a soldier and diplomat. They didn't judge, shout, manipulate, or punish. Instead, they taught peace through how they lived—with kindness, generosity, honesty, and mindfulness.

I was amazed. I wasn't just reading about peace—I was feeling it all around me.

Through their patient example, I began to see something important:

Peace isn't something you fight for or force. Peace is something you grow and nurture, like a beautiful lotus flower blooming from mud and murky water.

Even more profoundly, the monks helped me understand and reflect on the hidden roots of pain and human suffering: **greed, hatred, and ignorance.**

As they made clear;

Greed pulls us toward wanting more and more. Hatred pushes us to divide and hurt one another.

Ignorance—makes us forget how interconnected we truly are—keeps us trapped in fear and confusion.

These **three poisons**, as the monks called them, are like heavy stones we carry without even realizing it. But there is a way to put these stones of burden down.

The **Noble Eightfold Path** they lived and taught is a gentle, powerful way to heal our hearts and train our minds— to gradually replace greed with generosity, hatred with loving-kindness, and ignorance with understanding.

That's what this story is about: Learning to know your mind. Learning to walk a path of peace, happiness, and social harmony begins with knowing the mind and learning to see the world, and oneself, more clearly.

The contents of this storybook derive from a doctoral dissertation conducted with Theravāda Buddhist monks at Buddhism for Education of Cambodia (BEC). It is intended for children, families, teachers, and anyone who wonders if a better, kinder world is possible. It follows my journey learning from the monks in Cambodia—and how their peaceful way of living transformed the way I try to understand, think, speak, and act. Come join me on this exciting path. Let's walk gently, curiously, and mindfully together.

Foreword

✦

By His Eminence Dr. Yon Seng Yeath

With deep joy and respect, I write this foreword to honor Dr. Philip Keenan Abbott and his extraordinary gift to the Cambodian people: *The Journey of Curious Philip Ajere LaBier: A Storybook Inspired by the Noble Eightfold Path*

This storybook is not simply a book of words; it is a living testament to Philip's profound compassion, (Karunā) loving-kindness (mettā), and equanimity (upekkhā). In these pages, Philip offers a gift not for himself, but for the children, youth, teachers, and parents of Cambodia—a gift that springs from his heart's deep well of generosity and his commitment to inner and outer peace.

Through Philip's experience walking alongside the Theravāda Buddhist monks of Buddhism for Education of Cambodia (BEC) in post-genocide Cambodia, we encounter the timeless wisdom of the Noble Eightfold Path. Inspired by the humble yet mighty figures of Venerable Maha Ghosananda, Cambodia's great "Gandhi of the Mekong," and Odom Vansivon, whose simple faith introduced Philip to the living dhamma (Buddha's teaching), this book radiates the virtues of compassion, mindfulness, and peace.

This storybook does not teach peace as an idea only; it teaches peace as practice, a way of life, and a daily discipline. Through Philip's experience, readers—young and old alike—are invited to see that the true roots of peace are planted within, nourished by wise understanding, right thought, right speech, right action, and all the gentle steps of the Noble Path.

It is with great admiration that I commend Philip's insistence that this work be made available in both English and Khmer editions, ensuring accessibility to all levels of Cambodian education. Furthermore, Philip has expressed his wish that the English edition be included on the reading list within the Bachelor of Arts English Language curriculum. This speaks not only to his dedication to cross-cultural understanding but also to his faith in the power of education as a vehicle for peacebuilding and reconciliation.

As you turn these pages, may you feel the generosity of Philip's offering to the Cambodian people. May you be reminded of the strength that comes not from wealth or power, but from the quiet, patient work of transforming suffering into compassion, anger into loving-kindness, and confusion into wisdom.

I strongly recommend this storybook as essential for all—whether at the primary, secondary, or tertiary level. It is a beacon of light for the young, a reminder for adults, and a guide for all who walk the peaceful path.

May Philip's gift continue to water the seeds of peace in every heart and mind that reads this book.

With blessings of peace, happiness, and social harmony,
His Eminence Dr. Yon Seng Yeath,
Chancellor of Preah Sihanouk Raja Buddhist University

Message from the Rector

"In *The Journey of Curious Philip Ajere LaBier*, Dr. Abbott bridges cultures and wisdom in a way that nurtures understanding, compassion, and inner peace. This book is a rare gift—one that invites readers, young and old, to awaken not only their minds but also their hearts. Through his sincere collaboration with Theravāda Buddhist monks at Buddhism for Education of Cambodia (BEC), he offers a model of education rooted in morality, mindfulness, and loving-kindness.

I commend this storybook as a valuable contribution to peace education and to our collective journey toward harmony."

— Venerable Vy Sovechea
Rector, Preah Sihanouk Raja Buddhist University
Battambang, Cambodia

Introduction

The Curious Boy Who Wanted to Understand Peace, Happiness, and Social Harmony

He often asked questions like:

What is peace?

What makes people truly happy?

Why do some people live together in harmony, while others fight?

Why are there so many poor people in this world?

As he grew up, Philip became a soldier and a diplomat.

He wore a military uniform with medals and traveled to many countries.

He met leaders, solved problems, and gave speeches.

But still, something was missing inside his heart and mind.

He was searching for peace, happiness, and harmony, but he did not know where to find them.

One day, Philip traveled to a faraway country called the Kingdom of Cambodia.

It was a land of golden temples, kind people, and wise Buddhist monks.

These monks were not rich or famous.

They did not carry weapons or give long speeches.

They lived simply, with kindness, calmness, and respect for all living beings.

They helped others, shared what they had, and always smiled. Even in difficult times, their smiles came from the heart.

Philip was amazed.

He had searched for peace and happiness through power and success.

But the monks found peace by living with kindness and compassion.

So, Philip made a big decision.

He stayed in Cambodia, not to fight, but to learn a new way to live.

He wanted to understand how the monks created peace in their hearts and minds, and how that peace spread to others.

This book tells the story of his journey.

You will follow Philip as he learns about The Noble Eightfold Path, a peaceful way to live and grow.

Each chapter shares a story, a lesson, a journal reflection, and questions to help you think about how to live in peace, happiness, and harmony too.

Like a lotus flower rising from muddy water, we can grow something beautiful even from life's struggles.

Peace and happiness begin inside you, with one breath, one kind thought, and one gentle action at a time.

———— ✦ ————

The Noble Eightfold Path -A Simple and Practical Guide to Living Peacefully

The Noble Eightfold Path is like a map.

It shows us how to live with peace, kindness, and happiness.

It teaches us to treat others well, care for ourselves, and make the world a better place.

Here are the eight gentle steps:

Right Understanding (Sammā-diṭṭhi)

Seeing life clearly; understanding the Four Noble Truths and the law of cause and effect.

Right Thought (Sammā-saṅkappa)

Thinking kindly and wisely; intentions free from greed, hatred, and delusion.

Right Speech (Sammā-vācā)

Speaking truthfully, kindly, and helpfully; avoiding lies, gossip, or hurtful words.

Right Action (Sammā-kammanta)

Acting peacefully and ethically; refraining from harming living beings, stealing, or misconduct.

Right Livelihood (Sammā-ājīva)

Earning a living in ways that do not harm others; working with honesty and compassion.

Right Effort (Sammā-vāyāma)

Developing good qualities and letting go of unwholesome ones; practicing diligence.

Right Mindfulness (Sammā-sati)

Being fully aware and present in body, speech, and mind; observing thoughts without judgment.

Right Concentration (Sammā-samādhi)

Developing deep focus and calm through meditation; cultivating a peaceful and steady mind.

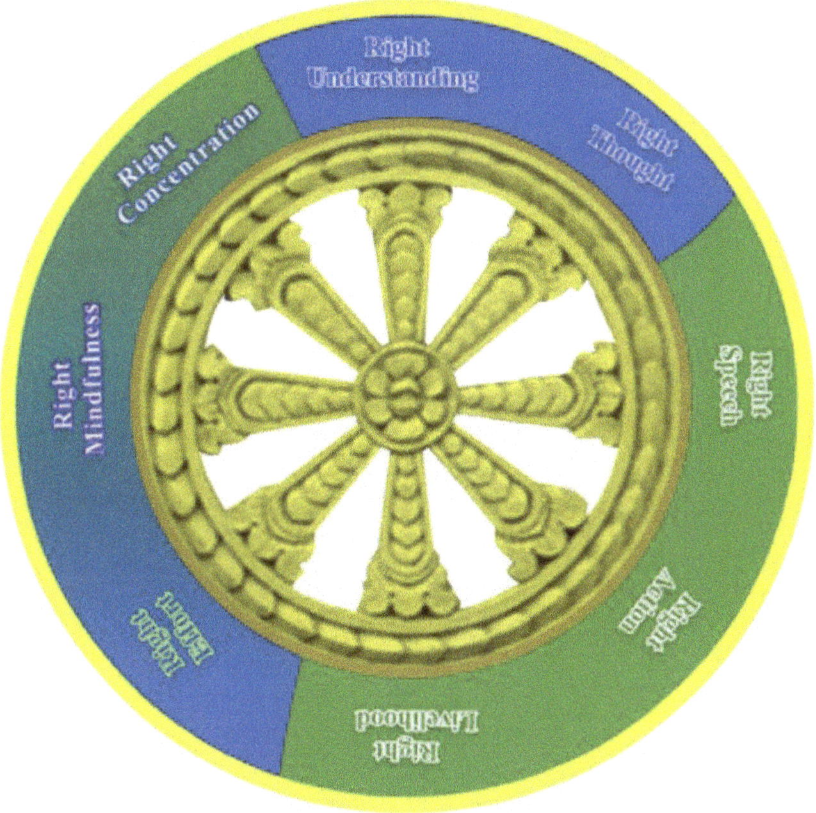

When we walk these 8 steps, we learn how to be wise, kind, and peaceful.

We grow happiness for ourselves and for others.

Just as a lotus flower needs water, sunlight, and care to grow, our minds need these steps to grow peace and joy.

When we follow them, we live a life filled with peace, happiness, and harmony.

SECTION ONE – WISDOM

—— ◆ ——

Welcome to the beginning of the journey: the wisdom path, or paññā. This is where Philip starts learning how to see clearly and think kindly.

In this section, we discover two very important steps:

- **Right Understanding** – seeing life as it really is

- **Right Thought** – planting good, kind thoughts in our minds

Philip learns that wisdom is not only about being smart or knowing answers. It is about looking at the world with open eyes and an open heart. It is about accepting that life is always changing, and that peace begins when we stop judging and start listening mindfully.

Sometimes, we rush to fix problems or blame others when we feel upset. But when we slow down and try to understand what is really happening, we can respond with kindness instead of anger.

Philip also learns that thoughts are like seeds. If we plant seeds of kindness, generosity, and love, good things will grow. If we allow harmful thoughts to take over, we may hurt others without even meaning to.

The monks in Cambodia teach Philip that wisdom begins inside us, with the way we see and think about the world.

Learning Focus of Section One

- To see life clearly and accept that things change.

- To think with compassion and let go of hurtful thoughts.

- To understand that peace begins with kind intentions and understanding.

Using the Teacher's Notes

The Teacher's Notes – Guiding the Lesson at the end of each chapter are designed to help teachers and parents translate the story's lessons into classroom and home learning.

While the Reflection Questions invite children to explore their feelings and ideas, the Teacher's Notes provide practical guidance to help educators nurture understanding, empathy, and social-emotional growth.

Each note highlights:

- ✹ Key teaching strategies that connect story themes with real-life practice.

- ✹ Mindful classroom activities encourage awareness, kindness, and reflection.

- ✹ Discussion approaches that model patience, listening, and compassion.

Teachers are encouraged to use the notes as a gentle guide, adapting examples and activities to their own classroom needs. The goal is not to deliver a lesson but to create a shared experience of learning peace — one that balances knowledge, moral awareness, and mindfulness.

When story and reflection meet with guided practice, children begin to see peace not as a distant idea, but as something they can live and share every day.

For extended classroom projects and thematic lessons, *see also* A Guide for Parents and Teachers (pp. 47-50).

Localization and Adaptation

The *Teacher's Notes* are intended for flexible use in diverse cultural and educational settings.

Teachers and facilitators are warmly encouraged to adapt the examples, language, and discussion themes to reflect local customs, traditions, and community experiences—while preserving the story's universal spirit of kindness, mindfulness, and understanding.

The spirit of the story is universal, but its expression can bloom uniquely in every classroom.

Chapter One
Right Understanding – Seeing the World Clearly

— ◆ —

Welcome to the Kingdom of Cambodia, where Philip's journey of understanding begins.

A land of golden temples, smiling faces, and quiet wisdom. Here, learning begins not just with the eyes, but with the heart and mind. This is where Philip's journey truly takes its first step.

Meet Philip! He isn't just any traveler. He came all the way from America, not for sightseeing or photographs, but to learn something far more meaningful—how to live in peace, happiness, and social harmony.

When he steps off the airplane, Philip is greeted by a group of gentle, smiling monks in bright orange robes. At the center stands **Venerable Hak Sienghai**, his hands holding a bouquet of fresh flowers.

"Welcome, Philip," says the monk with a warm smile. "You're not just here to look with your eyes. You're here to see with your heart and mind."

Philip smiles back, a little nervous but full of wonder. He climbs into a white van filled with cheerful monks and a kind driver named **Vuthy Vuthy**. As they zoom through the Cambodian countryside—past rice fields, palm trees, and buffalo—Philip sits quietly, taking it all in.

Everything feels different—but in a good way. The air feels peaceful. The land feels honest. The faces around him feel real.

Soon, they arrive at a temple in **Battambang Province**. The air is still. The only sounds are rustling leaves and the soft sweeping of monks cleaning the courtyard. Something inside Philip begins to shift. His mind, once restless with

questions, starts to slow and soften.

Under a great **Bodhi tree**—just like the one where the Buddha found enlightenment—Philip sits beside Venerable Hak Sienghai.

"Life is always changing," the monk says softly. "Sometimes we feel happy, sometimes we feel sad, and suffer. But when we understand that everything changes, we stop clinging so tightly. That is called **Right Understanding**."

Philip thinks back to times in his life when he tried to fix everything, like a superhero rushing in to save the day. But those quick fixes didn't always bring peace, happiness, or harmony.

Now, he wonders: *What if peace doesn't begin with fixing, but with understanding?*

Understanding that life isn't always fair. That people make mistakes. That nothing lasts forever. That no one is perfect. And perhaps… that is all right.

He takes a deep breath, and for the first time in a long while, he feels... free. Free of suffering.

From that moment on, Philip promises to practice seeing the world differently—not with judgment, but with mindfulness. Not to control it, but to understand it. Not to become attached to one way of thinking, but to welcome all thoughts.

"I once believed peace was something to fight for, but today I see it differently. I learned it is something softer. Life is always changing—people, moments, and even feelings are always shifting. When I stop clinging and start understanding with patience and care, my heart feels lighter, freer. True peace begins when I see the world as it really is—with clear eyes, a kind heart, and an open mind. Now I wonder: what kind of thoughts will help me carry this peace forward?"

Learning Objective

 To understand that life is always changing and nothing lasts forever.

 To learn that peace begins when we try to see clearly, listen with care, and accept change with kindness.

Reflection Questions

- Have you ever had a misunderstanding with a friend or family member? What happened?
- What helped you to understand their feelings or point of view?
- Can you think of a time when something made you sad at first, but later it helped you learn or grow stronger?
- How can you practice "seeing clearly" in your life today—at school, at home, or with friends?

Teacher's Notes – Guiding the Lesson for Right Understanding: Seeing the World Clearly

Guide students in exploring how perception shapes our relationships and emotions. Use storytelling or images that show how the same event can be seen in different ways. Encourage pausing before judgment and modeling empathy during discussions. Reinforce that "seeing clearly" means balancing what we know with how we feel, and welcoming many points of view.

For extended classroom projects and thematic lessons, see also A Guide for Parents and Teachers (pp. 47-50).

Chapter Two
Right Thought – Planting Seeds of Kindness

———— ✦ ————

The monks teach Philip that every kind thought is a seed of peace – planted with loving-kindness and watered with compassion.

Philip was riding in the white van with the smiling monks from Buddhism for Education of Cambodia. The morning sun was bright, and the air felt full of hope. They were on their way to visit a school in Battambang.

When they arrived, children in neat white shirts and blue skirts or pants ran toward the gates, waving and laughing. Their joy was infectious. They weren't simply greeting visitors. They were welcoming **teachers of peace**.

Inside the classroom, a kind monk named **Venerable Jaa Sam Saroun** held up a tiny seed.

He asked, "What will grow from this?"

"A flower!" shouted a girl in the front row.

"Yes," the monk said, "a beautiful flower. But it needs water, sunlight, and love to grow."

Then he smiled and said, "Our thoughts are just like this seed. If we take care of them—if we choose thoughts that are kind and gentle— they will grow into kind and gentle actions."

Philip listened closely.

He had never imagined his mind as a garden before, yet the image made perfect sense.

The monk continued, "Right Thought means choosing to think with love, compassion, and joy. It means letting go of angry, mean, or greedy thoughts—and planting thoughts that help others."

Philip sat very still. He looked inside his heart and mind. He asked himself:

"Have I planted seeds of kindness?" "Or seeds of anger and fear?"

Later that day, Philip helped the children clean the playground. As he picked up each piece of trash, he whispered a kind thought in his heart:

"May the earth be clean."

"May all children feel safe."

"May I be more patient and calm today."

"May people everywhere live in peace."

He wasn't just picking up litter.

With each small action, he was planting a peaceful garden inside his mind.

"My mind is like a garden, and each thought is like a seed. When I nurture kindness, generosity, and joy, they grow strong and make my heart feel light. Even one small kind thought can bloom into a forest of peace—spreading harmony and goodness to the world around me. When I choose peaceful intentions, I grow into a kinder person"

Learning Objective

- To understand that our thoughts are like seeds that grow into words and actions.
- To practice choosing kind, generous, and joyful thoughts that bring peace to ourselves and others.

Reflection Questions

- What kind of thoughts do you usually notice—are they kind, worried, or angry?
- Can you choose one kind thought right now and hold it gently, like a seed in your hand?
- How could that kind thought grow into kind words or actions today?
- If unkind thoughts are like weeds, how can you "pull them out" when they show up?

Teacher's Notes – Guiding the Lesson for Right Thought: Planting Seeds of Kindness

Invite students to imagine their minds as gardens of thought. Have them identify which thoughts help their learning and which distract or harm. Use art, drawing, or nature examples to visualize "planting" and "watering" kind intentions. Emphasize that teachers and students alike shape the classroom's emotional climate through the thoughts they choose to nurture.

For extended classroom projects and thematic lessons, see also A Guide for Parents and Teachers (pp. 47-50).

SECTION TWO – VIRTUE AND MORALITY

◆

*T*his part of the journey is about how we live in this interconnected world—how we talk, how we act, and the kind of work we choose to do.

It teaches us to:

- ◈ **Speak with loving-kindness and honesty** (Right Speech)

- ◈ **Do good things and avoid harm** (Right Action)

- ◈ **Choose jobs that help others, not hurt them** (Right Livelihood)

These three steps are part of living with virtue and morality, or what the monks call sīla.

When we speak kindly, act fairly, and work with love and compassion, we help create a more peaceful world—for ourselves and for everyone around us. This is what the monks in Cambodia practice every day. It is the essence of their peace education program, and it shows how small choices in daily life can shape harmony for all.

Chapter Three
Right Speech – The Power of Words

— ✦ —

Philip learns to connect with others by using truthful, kind, and helpful words.

Philip stood quietly at the edge of a schoolyard in Cambodia. Children sat in neat rows on colorful mats, their hands folded in respect. The breeze was soft, and sunlight filtered gently through the trees.

At the front stood a peaceful monk named **Venerable Yem Vanna**. He wore a bright orange robe and held a small microphone. The children listened silently.

One little boy stood up to speak. But his voice shook, and he sat down quickly, looking sad.

Venerable Yem Vanna walked over, knelt beside him, and said gently, "It's okay to make mistakes. No one is perfect. What matters is how we speak—to others and to ourselves."

Then he spoke to everyone:

"Right Speech means using words that are kind, true, and helpful."

Our words can lift people up, or they can bring people down. Let's choose words that bring joy to this world we all live in."

Philip watched closely. The monk spoke with such ease—not loudly, never with anger. His voice was steady and calm, carrying a warmth that comforted everyone listening.

Later that evening, Philip sat near a quiet pond. Venerable Yem Vanna was there too, scattering bits of food into the water for the fish.

Philip watched the ripples spreading outward, each one touching another. He thought, "Words are like ripples. They travel far. I want my words to carry far too, and to travel peacefully."

He remembered times when he had not been truthful, when he had spoken in anger or with harshness. The memory weighed on him, and he felt sorry.

In that moment, he made a promise to himself: "I will let my words heal, not hurt. I will speak like the monks do—with calm, care, and kindness."

"Words are powerful and lasting. They can bring people together or push them apart. When I choose words that are gentle, truthful, and kind, they become bridges of peace. Each kind word I speak helps me grow into a kinder person and makes the world feel more connected."

Learning Objective

 To learn that words can heal or hurt, connect or divide.

 To practice speaking with kindness, honesty, and respect so our words become bridges of peace.

Reflection Questions

- Can you remember a time when someone's words made you feel really good—or really hurt inside? What happened?
- How do your words make other people feel—like sunshine or like something else?
- What are some kind and truthful words you can practice using every day?
- If words are like ripples that spread out, what kind of ripples do you want your words to create?

Teacher's Notes – Guiding the Lesson for Right Speech: The Power of Words

Model compassionate communication by exploring tone, timing, and truthfulness. Create short role-plays where students practice turning negative or careless words into helpful, kind phrases. Introduce a "kind words wall" or classroom mantra that celebrates respectful language. Reinforce that speaking truth with kindness builds trust and belonging.

For extended classroom projects and thematic lessons, see also A Guide for Parents and Teachers (pp. 47-50).

Chapter Four
Right Action – Living with Morality

— ✦ —

The monks show Philip what generosity means by
building a house—with kindness in their hearts and
smiles on their faces.

One sunny morning, Philip joined the monks on a journey to a small village. The bright green rice fields shimmered in the sunlight as farmers worked patiently in the heat.

When they arrived, children ran out giggling, and elders waved with warm smiles. A family needed help building their new home, and the monks had come not with fancy tools but with open hearts, willing hands, and joyful spirits.

Philip didn't hesitate. He picked up a hammer and began working side by side with the monks and neighbors. Children carried buckets of water. Grandparents stirred big pots of rice. Some people swept the yard while others brought bamboo poles. Everyone had a role. No one was left out.

As they worked, **Venerable Hak Sienghai** turned to Philip and said, "Right Action—or Kamma in the Pali language—means doing what is kind and good. It means not hurting others, not taking what isn't yours, and always being honest. Even the smallest act of kindness, like a smile, can help build peace."

As Philip nailed a wooden board into place, he paused. He realized he wasn't just helping to build a house. He was building something inside himself too—a life rooted in kindness, compassion, and joy.

That night, Philip sat quietly with the monks. The stars sparkled overhead, and the crickets sang across the rice fields.

He thought to himself: *Helping feels better than wanting. Being kind feels stronger than being right.*

"Today I felt strong—not because I used force, but because I chose compassion, kindness, and joy. I gave my time. I helped with love. I also learned that kindness is more than a feeling. It is something we build with our hands and live through our choices. Helping others is the strongest action of all. I wonder if the way I live and work each day can also be a path to peace?"

Learning Objective

- To understand that our actions—big or small—shape the kind of world we live in.
- To practice making choices that are fair, kind, and helpful, even when it is difficult.

Reflection Questions

- Can you remember one kind thing you did recently? How did it make you feel?
- What is one small kind action you could do today—at home, at school, or in your community?
- Sometimes we face choices: to help or walk away, to tell the truth or hide it. What helps you choose the kinder action?
- If every kind action is like building a brick in a house of peace, what kind of house are you building?

Teacher's Notes – Guiding the Lesson for Right Action: Living with Morality

Use this chapter to connect ethical choices with community well-being. Encourage students to brainstorm small, achievable class service actions—cleaning shared spaces, helping a classmate, or showing gratitude. Afterward, guide a reflection on how kind actions strengthen confidence and cooperation. Highlight that peace grows through doing good, not just knowing what is good.

For extended classroom projects and thematic lessons, see also A Guide for Parents and Teachers (pp. 47-50).

Chapter Five
Right Livelihood – A Kind Way to Live

*Philip learns to make choices that help others—because
every step matters when walking the peaceful path.*

In Cambodia, Philip learned many things. But one of the greatest lessons came when he visited a school where monks were teaching older children about choosing kind and helpful jobs.

He sat quietly in the back of the classroom as a monk pointed to the chalkboard. It read:

Right Livelihood = Work that helps, not harms.

The monk explained, "Some jobs make the world better—like being a teacher, a doctor, or protecting nature. But some jobs bring harm to people or the planet. Right Livelihood means choosing work that spreads kindness, peace, and happiness."

After class, Philip met Khien Kimsong, a former monk who had once taught insight meditation in prisons as part of a rehabilitation program. He shared how guiding people behind bars to breathe calmly and reflect helped them discover peace inside themselves. Today, Kimsong is a layperson and no longer participates in the prisoner education program.

Kimsong explained that in Cambodia, there is a growing need for this kind of peace education. Many people in prison want to learn meditation, but there are not enough monks to visit all the prisons. The monks believe this work matters deeply because true change comes from helping people heal—not from punishment alone.

Philip listened with deep respect. He had never thought of prisons as places where peace could grow, but Kimsong showed him it was possible.

"Fear makes people grab and take," Kimsong said softly. "But love does the opposite. Love helps us give, listen, and care."

Those words stayed with Philip. He realized he had once believed power and control made the world safe. But now, he could see that love was the true source of safety.

Later, they walked through a village where children laughed and played. Some dreamed of becoming teachers, artists, or doctors. They weren't just dreaming about careers—they were dreaming with love.

Kimsong pointed to a young girl painting a colorful mural on the school wall.

"That's love in action," he said with a smile.

Philip nodded, feeling his heart lighten.

"Maybe peace isn't only something we talk about," he thought. "Maybe it's something we live—one kind act, one kind choice at a time."

"I used to think a job was only about earning money and gaining power. But now I understand—it is about helping others. When I work with compassion and kindness, I feel alive. When I add joy, I feel truly happy. Still, kind work alone is not enough. I must also train my mind each day to keep peace growing. I wonder—how can I keep planting seeds of kindness in myself and in the world?"

Learning Objective

- To learn that the kind of work we choose can help people, animals, and the planet.

- To see that real success comes from work that spreads peace, kindness, and joy.

Reflection Questions

- What job or role would you like when you grow up, and why does it interest you?
- How could that job help people, animals, or the planet?
- Even as a student, what kind of "work" can you do now that spreads kindness and peace?
- Some jobs bring harm, while others bring healing. How can we learn to tell the difference?

Teacher's Notes – Guiding the Lesson for Right Livelihood: A Kind Way to Live

Help students link personal responsibility to compassion in everyday choices. Facilitate discussion on how different jobs or tasks contribute to society's well-being. Use examples—from teachers and farmers to environmental caretakers and nurses—to show that meaningful work serves life rather than harms it. Encourage curiosity about how each person's daily actions can embody kindness and integrity.

For extended classroom projects and thematic lessons, see also A Guide for Parents and Teachers (pp. 47-50).

SECTION THREE – MINDFULNESS

◆

Right Effort –
Right Mindfulness –
Right Concentration

The journey continues...

Philip had already learned so much—how to think kindly, speak gently, and act with compassion. Now it was time for a new part of the journey: learning how to calm his mind and care for his heart.

This part of the journey was quieter. It wasn't about building houses or sharing meals—it was about noticing each moment, one breath at a time.

With the monks, Philip learned to sweep the ground slowly, walk with care, and sit in stillness. He saw children breathing deeply, letting go of worries, and allowing peace to grow inside them.

Philip realized something important: peace doesn't just come from what we do. It also comes from how we pay attention to our thoughts, feelings, and actions.

Mindfulness means trying your best, noticing what is happening right now, and being calm and focused like a still pond. That's how peace grows—within us, and then outward into the world.

Practicing meditation, Philip discovered, is not about escaping the world. It is about becoming familiar with your own mind and learning to live in harmony with it.

Chapter Six
Right Effort – Growing Goodness Every Day

———— ✦ ————

*Philip learns that every mindful effort—like almsgiving—
is a seed of generosity that blossoms into compassion and
sympathetic joy.*

One quiet morning, Philip woke up early and followed the monks outside. The sun was just rising, and the temple grounds were cool and still. He saw the monks sweeping the stone paths with straw brooms.

Venerable Yem Vanna smiled and said, "We sweep not just the dust from the ground, but also the dust from our minds."

Philip liked that thought. It made him wonder how to sweep away the unhelpful thoughts in his mind and begin each day fresh.

The monks explained that Right Effort means trying your best to grow good thoughts and let go of harmful ones. It's like tending a garden: water the flowers, not the weeds.

Later that day, Philip visited a school where children sat quietly in meditation. Their eyes were closed, their breathing steady, their minds calm.

One child opened his eyes and said, "I'm trying to be more patient today."

Another said, "I want to stop being mean to my little brother."

Philip felt proud of them. He realized Right Effort wasn't about being perfect. It was about trying, practicing, and starting again each day with kindness.

"Every day is a chance to begin again. By sweeping away harmful thoughts and planting seeds of kindness, I can grow a peaceful heart. This effort feels gentle, like watering a garden. I wonder—how can I stay mindful so that these seeds of goodness keep growing strong?"

Learning Objective

- To understand that no one is perfect, but we can try each day to grow good habits.

- To practice "watering the flowers" of kindness, patience, and joy while letting go of harmful thoughts and habits.

Reflection Questions

- What is one good habit or skill you are practicing or want to get better at?

- What is one unhelpful habit you would like to let go of—like pulling a weed from your garden?

- How can you remind yourself each day to "water the flowers" of kindness, patience, or joy?

- When you make a mistake, what helps you try again with kindness instead of giving up?

Teacher's Notes – Guiding the Lesson for Right Effort: Growing Goodness Every Day

Focus on perseverance and mindful discipline rather than perfection. Encourage students to set gentle daily goals—acts of patience, cooperation, or gratitude—and celebrate progress together. When frustration arises, guide breathing pauses or quiet moments of awareness. Emphasize that genuine effort is steady, joyful, and renewed with each new day.

For extended classroom projects and thematic lessons, see also A Guide for Parents and Teachers (pp. 47-50).

Chapter Seven
Right Mindfulness – Living in the Present

Practicing meditation is a powerful way of getting to know yourself and becoming familiar with your mind.

One sunny afternoon, Philip joined the monks on a quiet walk through the temple garden. They moved slowly, one step at a time. Philip noticed the warm sun on his face, the chirping birds in the trees, and the gentle crunch of leaves under his feet.

"This is called mindfulness," said Venerable Yem Vanna. "It means paying attention to the present moment—to what we see, hear, smell, and feel right now."

Philip realized that his mind often wandered, worrying about the future or feeling sad about the past. But when he brought his attention back to the present moment, he felt calm and at peace.

Later, Philip watched the children during a mindfulness session using insight (vipassanā) meditation. They sat quietly, eyes closed, breathing in and out. Some of the children had tears on their cheeks, yet their faces looked lighter and more at ease.

Philip smiled. He understood that **Right Mindfulness** was not about being serious or silent all the time. It was about being fully awake and alive in each moment.

"When I am still, I can feel my breath and the calmness inside me. I do not have to hold on to the past, and I do not have to race toward the future. Peace is already here, like sunshine warming my heart. Living in the present makes me feel awake and alive. I am learning that I can recognize the past and the future, and at the same time concentrate on being fully in the present—where peace grows stronger."

Learning Objective

 To learn how to notice what is happening in the present moment without being pulled away by past or future worries.

 To practice paying attention with calmness and curiosity—using our senses, breath, and awareness.

Reflection Questions

* If you sit quietly for one minute, what sounds, smells, and feelings can you notice around you?
* What thoughts come into your mind when you are still? Can you watch them float by like clouds in the sky?
* How does your body feel when you are paying attention to the present moment? Calm? Restless? Happy?
* What is one small thing you can do each day to remind yourself to be mindful—like breathing before speaking or noticing the sunshine?

Teacher's Notes – Guiding the Lesson for Right Mindfulness: Living in the Present

Introduce mindfulness as a skill that improves attention and empathy. Lead short awareness breaks during class transitions—listening to sounds, feeling the breath, or noticing one thing to appreciate. Connect mindfulness to calm decision-making and emotional regulation. Reinforce that awareness allows students to respond wisely rather than react impulsively.

For extended classroom projects and thematic lessons, see also A Guide for Parents and Teachers (pp. 47-50).

Chapter Eight
Right Concentration – Finding Inner Peace

— ✦ —

Sacred spaces can inspire deep focus and spiritual reflection.

At a quiet school in Battambang, Philip joined a large group of students sitting in a circle. They were preparing for something very special: meditation. The students sat on mats, closed their eyes, and began to breathe slowly, just as the monks had taught them.

Venerable Jaa Sam Saroun spoke gently. "Let your mind be still, like a calm pond. When our minds are peaceful, we can see everything clearly."

Some students smiled, some cried softly, but all of them sat very still, following their breaths with care. Philip sat beside them and did the same. He felt his thoughts slow down, drifting gently like leaves on water.

He realized something wonderful. He didn't need to rush or fix everything, and he didn't need all the answers. He only needed to be still and breathe. That was the gift of Right Concentration.

The following day, as he walked near the lotus pond outside Angkor Wat, Philip paused. The water was so still that it reflected the clouds above. "That is what my heart feels like," he thought. "Still, open, and full of peace."

"When I sit quietly and follow my breath, my mind begins to settle, like a pond growing still. Thoughts about the past or the future sometimes appear. I can notice them, learn from them, and gently return to the present moment. In this calmness, I begin to see more clearly and to hold kinder thoughts and understanding. With practice, I can choose to rest my mind on kindness, generosity, and wisdom. This makes my heart feel lighter, happier, and full of peace. Through insight meditation—learning to see clearly inside my mind—peace grows stronger, one breath and one kind thought at a time."

Learning Objective

- To learn how to calm and focus the mind through stillness and breathing.

- To understand that concentration helps us see clearly inside, making space for peace, kindness, and wisdom to grow.

Reflection Questions

- What helps you stay focused when you are learning something new or doing something important?
- Can you think of a time when your mind felt calm and steady, like a still pond? What were you doing?
- How does focusing on your breath or one kind thought make you feel inside?
- When your mind wanders, how can you gently bring it back to calm and focus?

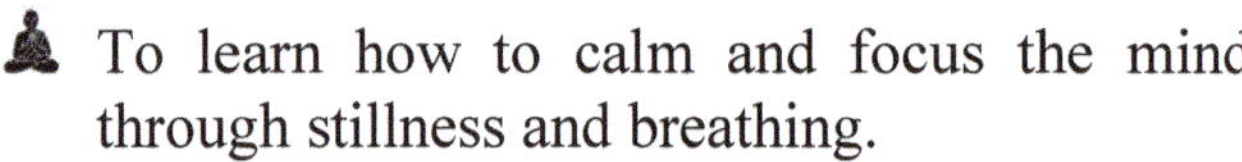

Teacher's Notes – Guiding the Lesson for Right Concentration: Finding Inner Peace

Help students experience deep focus through quiet, enjoyable exercises. Begin with one-minute concentration practice—watching a candle flame, following the breath, or observing a natural object. Discuss how focus brings clarity and peace to both learning and life. Encourage students to see concentration not as effortful silence but as relaxed awareness of the present moment.

For extended classroom projects and thematic lessons, see also A Guide for Parents and Teachers (pp. 47-50).

Conclusion
A Journey of Peace That Starts Inside Your Mind

—◆—

During his time with the monks at Buddhism for Education of Cambodia, Philip had walked the Noble Eightfold Path. He had learned how to see clearly, think kindly, speak gently, act with love, choose a helpful job, try his best, stay in the moment, and focus his mind.

He discovered that peace is not something we find outside. It is something we grow inside ourselves, one kind choice at a time.

As Philip waved goodbye to the monks, the children, and the golden temples, he smiled. Their lessons would stay with him forever, like a soothing song in his heart. And just like that, the journey goes on. One breath. One step. One kind thought at a time.

Philip wrote in his journal: *"I used to think peace, happiness, and social harmony were something outside of me, now I know—it starts inside our mind and heart."*

Final Reflection Questions:

- **Which part of the Eightfold Path do you want to practice more?**

- **How can it help you and others make this world a peaceful, happy, and harmonious place?**

A Guide for Parents and Teachers

This Teaching Guide is designed to help parents and teachers explore the **Noble Eightfold Path** with children through reflection, discussion, and simple practices. Each chapter includes learning objectives and reflection questions, and this guide extends the learning with activities and key concepts.

Teaching Tips by Chapter

Chapter 1: Right Understanding

- ✹ Discuss how misunderstandings happen.

- ✹ Role-play scenarios where kids must stop and think before reacting.

- ✹ Help children understand that change and challenge are part of life.

Chapter 2: Right Thought

- ✹ Practice a "kind thoughts" circle: each person says one kind thought for another.

- ✹ Have children draw or journal one way they can be more generous.

Chapter 3: Right Speech

- ✹ Create a "mindful words" chart with examples of kind and unkind speech.

- ✹ Read a story or scenario and ask: "What would be the mindful way to speak?"

Chapter 4: Right Action

- ✹ Plan a class or family kindness project.

- ✹ Brainstorm good deeds children can do every day.

Chapter 5: Right Livelihood

- ✹ Talk about different kinds of jobs and how some help people.

- ✳ Ask children what they want to be when they grow up and how it could help others.

Chapter 6: Right Effort

- ✳ Use a chart to track when kids try their best each day.

- ✳ Teach children to notice when they're slipping into bad habits and gently guide them back.

- ✳ Encourage children to develop language for good and unhelpful moments, and practice naming them.

Chapter 7: Right Mindfulness

- ✳ Practice a few minutes of quiet breathing before class or bedtime.

- ✳ Take a mindful nature walk and describe what they see, hear, smell, and feel.

Chapter 8: Right Concentration

- ✳ Play a concentration game like focusing on one sound or object.

- ✳ Try short meditation or quiet sitting time.

Suggested Reflection Prompts

- What does peace mean to you?

- How can we show kindness when someone is upset?

- What helps you calm your mind?

Additional Activities

- Make a "Peace Poster" using images and words from each chapter.

- Create a Noble Eightfold Path wheel or chart.

- Have children interview a grandparent or elder about what brings them peace, happiness, and social harmony.

Final Notes

—— ✦ ——

This storybook is not only a journey through Buddhist teachings (dhamma). It is also a path toward emotional growth, peaceful habits, and meaningful reflection for learners of all ages. Encourage curiosity, generosity, and remind children that peace, happiness, and social harmony begin inside each of us. It is a step-by-step adventure.

The Journey of Curious Philip Ajere LaBier By Colonel (Ret.) Philip K. Abbott, Ph.D.

Based on real-life experiences and research with Theravāda Buddhist monks in post-genocide Cambodia.

Glossary of Terms

Ajere: A Yoruba name from Western Africa, meaning "one who brings good to others."

Almsgiving: A Buddhist practice of offering food, gifts, or support to monks or people in need. It shows kindness, generosity, and humility.

Angkor Wat: A famous and sacred temple complex in Cambodia, known as a symbol of spiritual and cultural heritage.

Battambang Province: A peaceful area in northwestern Cambodia where Philip studied with kind and wise monks.

Bodhi Tree: A sacred tree where the Buddha is believed to have become enlightened. It represents wisdom and spiritual awakening.

Cambodia: A Southeast Asian country with rich Buddhist traditions and kind-hearted people, where Philip's peaceful journey takes place.

Clearly: In a way that is easy to understand, see, or hear.

Compassion *(Karuṇā)*: A strong feeling of care that makes you want to help others who are suffering.

Concentration *(Samādhi)*: Focusing your mind calmly, like a still pond.

Connect: To join with someone or something in a kind, caring, or meaningful way.

Cultivate: To help something grow, such as peace or kindness, by caring for it with patience and love.

Curious: Wanting to learn and explore more about the world around you.

Delusion *(Moha)*: A form of ignorance that prevents the understanding of truth.

Dhamma: The Buddha's teachings that guide people to live wisely, morally, and mindfully.

Diplomat: Someone who works to build peace and understanding between countries through communication and respect.

Divide: To separate into parts or to make people feel apart from one another.

Dukkha: The truth of suffering.

Equanimity *(Upekkhā)*: Maintaining calm and balance in all situations.

Essence: The true, important nature of something—what it really is deep inside.

Explore: To go on an adventure or journey to learn new things.

Four Sublime States *(Brahmavihāras)*: The path to inner peace and lasting happiness.

- Loving-Kindness (Mettā): Universal goodwill

- ❋ Compassion (Karuṇā): Care for suffering

- ❋ Sympathetic Joy (Muditā): Joy in others' happiness

- ❋ Equanimity (Upekkhā): Wise balance and calm

Four Noble Truths:

- ❋ The truth of suffering. (dukkha)

- ❋ The truth of the cause of suffering. (craving and attachment)

- ❋ The truth of the cessation of suffering. (nirvana)

- ❋ The truth of the path to the end of suffering. (the noble eightfold path)

Focus: To give full attention to one thing at a time.

Generosity *(Dāna)*: The act of giving freely with a kind heart, without expecting anything in return.

Genesis: The beginning or start of something new, like a journey or idea.

Gentle: Being soft, kind, and calm in how you speak or act.

Grateful: Feeling thankful and happy for what you have or receive.

Greed *(Lobha)*: When we keep wanting more, even when we already have enough.

Harmony: Living together peacefully and respectfully, without conflict.

Hatred *(Dosa)*: When our heart closes, and we see others as enemies instead of fellow human beings.

Honesty: Telling the truth and being fair in your words and actions.

Humility: Knowing you are not better than others and treating everyone with respect.

Insight *(Vipassanā)***:** Learning to see clearly inside your own mind and the world we all live in.

Journey: A trip or adventure where you discover, grow, and learn.

Judge: To make a quick decision or opinion about someone, sometimes without enough understanding.

Kamma: Wholesome or unwholesome action.

Kindness: Being warm, caring, and thoughtful to others. (Pāli: Mettā)

LaBier: A French surname traditionally referred to someone who carried **goods, responsibilities, or messages**, or metaphorically, someone entrusted with something important.

Loving-Kindness *(Mettā)*: Wishing good things for others, just as you would for yourself.

Meditation: A peaceful practice of calming your mind and focusing on your breath or thoughts to understand yourself better.

Mindfulness: Paying close attention to what is happening right now without judging. (Right Mindfulness: Sammā Sati)

Monk: A person who dedicates their life to spiritual learning,

often living simply and teaching kindness and wisdom.

Moral Conduct *(Sīla)*: Living in a way that is ethical, kind, and respectful toward others—through our speech, actions, and livelihood.

Morality *(Sīla)*: The way we live that shows respect, kindness, and honesty toward others.

Muditā: A joyful feeling that arises when we see others happy or doing well.

Noble Eightfold Path: The Buddha's guide to living Wisely, Morally, and Mindfully.

Patient: Able to wait calmly without getting upset or angry.

Peace: A feeling of calm, happiness, and balance inside yourself and with others.

Philip Ajere LaBier: A name that quietly carries a layered meaning: *A friend and traveler who brings and carries good into the world.*

Poison: Something harmful, not only to the body, but also to the mind—like anger, greed, or ignorance.

Poor: Having little money or possessions, but still able to show kindness and love.

Promise: A commitment or agreement to do something or act in a certain way.

Rich: Having many things like money, but not always happiness or peace.

Right Action: Choosing to do kind and fair things without

hurting anyone. (Sammā Kammanta)

Right Concentration: Focusing your mind peacefully and clearly through meditation. (Sammā Samādhi)

Right Effort: Trying your best to grow good thoughts and let go of harmful ones. (Sammā Vāyāma)

Right Livelihood: Choosing work that helps others and avoids harm. (Sammā Ājīva)

Right Mindfulness: Paying attention to your thoughts, feelings, and actions with care. (Sammā Sati)

Right Speech: Using words that are truthful, kind, and helpful. (Sammā Vācā)

Right Thought: Thinking in loving, peaceful, and helpful ways. (Sammā Saṃkappa)

Right Understanding: Seeing life clearly and accepting change. (Sammā Diṭṭhi)

Sad: Feeling unhappy or suffering inside your heart and mind.

Soldier: A person who serves and protects their country, often with strength and discipline.

Spiritual: Connected to deep thoughts, feelings, and the search for life's deeper meaning.

Superhero: Someone (real or imagined) who helps others and stands up for what is good.

Sympathetic Joy *(Muditā)*: Delighting in others' joy.

Temple: A sacred place where monks live, practice, and

teach peace and mindfulness.

Theravāda Buddhism: An ancient form of Buddhism that focuses on wisdom, mindfulness, and living ethically. Common in Cambodia and Southeast Asia. Commonly practiced in Cambodia, Laos, Myanmar (Burma), Sri Lanka, and Thailand.

Transformation: A big and beautiful change that helps someone or something grow and improve.

Trash: Things thrown away because they are no longer useful—can also mean harmful thoughts we let go of.

Venerable: A respectful title given to a monk who lives with deep wisdom and compassion.

Vipassanā: A special kind of meditation that helps you understand your thoughts and experiences clearly. (Pāli for 'insight')

Wisdom *(Paññā)*: A deep understanding that helps us see clearly, make kind choices, and reduce suffering.

Vocabulary Workshop

This workshop helps children explore important words from the storybook. Activities include fun games, discussions, and group exercises that build understanding, kindness, and teamwork.

Part 1: Match the Word (with Clues!)

Using the Glossary of Terms (Pages 52-57), match each word to its meaning. Try using your imagination to think of a clue or picture for each one!

Example:

1. Almsgiving

2. Angkor Wat

3. Battambang Province

4. Bodhi Tree

5. Cambodia

6. Clearly

7. Compassion

8. Concentration

9. Connect

10. Cultivate

Now match them to these meanings:

1. A Buddhist practice of giving food, gifts, or help to monks or others in need. It is a way to show kindness, generosity, and humility.

2. A famous and sacred temple complex in Cambodia, known as a symbol of spiritual and cultural heritage.

3. A peaceful area in northwestern Cambodia where Philip learns from kind and wise monks.

4. A sacred tree where the Buddha is believed to have become enlightened. It represents wisdom and spiritual awakening.

5. A Southeast Asian country with rich Buddhist traditions and kind- hearted people, where Philip's peaceful journey takes place.

6. In a way that is easy to understand, see, or hear.

7. A strong feeling of care that makes you want to help others who are suffering. (Pāli: Karuṭā)

8. Focusing your mind calmly and deeply, often through meditation, to find peace inside. (Right Concentration – Sammā Samādhi)

9. To join with someone or something in a kind, caring, or meaningful way.

10. To help something grow, like peace or kindness, by caring for it with patience and love.

Part 2: Fill in the Blank

Choose the best word from the Glossary of Terms to complete each sentence. Use each word only once.

Example:

Curious, Dhamma, Diplomat, Divide, Essence, Explore, Focus, Generosity, Genesis, Gentle

1. Wanting to learn and explore more about the world around you.

2. The teachings of the Buddha that guide people to live wisely, kindly, and peacefully.

3. Someone who works to build peace and understanding between countries through communication and respect.

4. To separate into parts or to cause people to feel apart from one another.

5. The true, important nature of something—what makes it what it is deep down.

6. To go on an adventure or journey to learn new things.

7. To give full attention to one thing at a time.

8. The act of giving freely with a kind heart, without expecting anything in return. (Pāli: Dāna)

9. The beginning or start of something new, like a journey or idea.

10. Being soft, kind, and calm in how you speak or act.

Part 3: Group Story Game

In small groups, pick five vocabulary words. Together, create a short story using all five words. Make sure the story teaches a lesson about peace, kindness, or understanding. Then draw a picture of one scene from your story!

Part 4: Act It Out!

Pick a vocabulary word and act it out for the class (like charades). Can your friends guess the word? Then explain why this word is important to the story of Curious Philip.

Part 5: Word of the Day Journals

Each day, choose one word from the glossary. In your journal, write what the word means, how you can show it in real life, and draw a picture of someone practicing it.

Example:

Word: Kindness

Meaning: Being nice and caring.

How I show it: I helped my friend clean up today! Picture: (Draw a scene of kindness!)

About the Author

Philip Keenan Abbott, Ph.D., born Philip Ajere LaBier in New York, is a retired United States Army Colonel, former diplomat, peace scholar, and educator. He has dedicated his life to service first in uniform, later in diplomacy, and now through peace training and teaching.

Dr. Abbott earned a Bachelor of Arts in International Studies and Spanish from Norwich University, a Master of

Arts in Latin American Studies from Kansas University, a Master of Science in National Policy and Strategy from the National War College, and a Ph.D. in Conflict Analysis and Resolution from George Mason University's Carter School.

Commissioned as a Second Lieutenant in the Infantry, Dr. Abbott later became a Latin American Foreign Area Officer, serving in multiple U.S. embassies and leading humanitarian and security programs around the world. After retiring from a 33-year career in government service, he pursued a deeper understanding of inner peace and social harmony.

His doctoral research, a participatory action study with socially engaged Theravāda Buddhist monks in post-genocide Cambodia, became the foundation for this storybook. Living and learning with these monks transformed his worldview and taught him the profound value of wisdom, morality, and mindfulness in building peace.

Dr. Abbott has taught Interpersonal Conflict Resolution at George Mason University and English Communications at Preah Sihanouk Raja Buddhist University in Battambang, Cambodia, where he continues to walk alongside those committed to healing and cultivating harmony. He currently lives between the United States and Switzerland with his beloved wife, Maya, whose name, like the mother of the Buddha, reminds him daily of life's spiritual unfolding.

Who am I, Really?

- Am I greedy, or am I generous?
- Am I hateful, or am I kind and compassionate?
- Am I delusional (ignorant), or am I wise?

Appendix: Teacher's Guide to The Journey of Curious Philip Ajere LaBier

Integrating Peace Education Through Story and Reflection

Purpose of this Guide

This appendix supports teachers, parents, and facilitators in using *The Journey of Curious Philip Ajere LaBier* to nurture understanding, compassion, and mindfulness in learners. Grounded in the **Threefold Training**—Wisdom (*paññā*), Morality (*sīla*), and Mindfulness (*samādhi*)—the guide links story experiences to the **Noble Eightfold Path** and modern peace-education practice.

I. Learning Framework

Core Buddhist Pillar	Classroom Focus	Key Learning Outcomes
Wisdom (*Paññā*)	Critical thinking and self-understanding	Students recognize causes of conflict and identify peaceful responses.
Morality (*Sīla*)	Ethical living and empathy	Students practice right speech, right action, and respect for diversity.
Mindfulness (*Samādhi*)	Awareness and emotional regulation	Students apply mindful breathing and reflection to daily life.

Pedagogical Approach: *Experience → Reflection → Understanding → Action* (adapted from participatory action research and Buddhist experiential learning).

II. Using the Storybook in Class

1. Before Reading

- Begin with a **silent moment of breathing** (30 seconds) to settle attention.

- Introduce "Philip" as a real learner discovering peace through everyday experiences.

- Ask: *What does curiosity mean? When have you learned something through kindness?*

2. During Reading

- Read each chapter aloud or in small groups.

- Pause for journal moments: invite students to note a feeling, question, or insight.

- Encourage connection between the story's setting (Cambodia) and local community experiences.

3. After Reading Each Chapter

Use the built-in **Learning Objectives** and **Reflection Questions** plus these extension activities:

Chapter Focus	Suggested Classroom Activity	Cross-Curricular Link
Right View – Seeing Clearly	Students illustrate "what peace looks like" in their community.	Art & Civics
Right Thought – Planting Seeds of Wisdom	Group planting activity symbolizing intention; discuss caring for growth.	Science & Ethics
Right Speech – Speaking Truthfully	Role-play resolving a classroom disagreement using kind words.	Language Arts
Right Action – Living Responsibly	Community-cleanup or recycling project.	Environmental Studies
Right Livelihood – Working with Purpose	Interview a family member about meaningful work.	Social Studies
Right Effort – Persevering Mindfully	Journal about overcoming a personal challenge.	SEL (Social-Emotional Learning)
Right Mindfulness – Living Presently	Practice guided mindful breathing for one minute daily.	Health & Wellness
Right Concentration – Finding Inner Peace	Quiet reflection drawing or poem writing.	Creative Writing

III. Assessment and Reflection Tools

1. **Peace Journal**

    o Students record weekly reflections: "What did I practice this week—generosity, patience, understanding?"

2. **Compassion Circle**

    o End-of-week dialogue where each student shares one act of kindness they observed or offered.

3. **Mindful Observation Rubric**

Criteria	Emerging	Developing	Practicing	Exemplary
Self-awareness				
Respectful speech				
Cooperative behavior				

IV. Connecting to the Curriculum

- **UNESCO Global Citizenship & Peace Education Goals:** empathy, respect, conflict resolution, global awareness.

- **Social-Emotional Learning (CASEL) Competencies:** self-management, relationship skills, responsible decision-making.

- **Moral Education Outcomes:** aligning intentions, speech, and actions toward non-harm (*ahiṃsā*).

V. Extended Projects

1. **"Letters to Philip"** – students write letters offering advice or reflections on his journey.

2. **"Our Peace Path" Mural** – class paints the Eightfold Path as a spiral mural linking school and community life.

3. **Family Dialogue Night** – students share journal entries with parents, fostering intergenerational learning.

VI. Teacher Reflection

"To teach peace is to live peace."
After each session, note:

- What emotions surfaced?

- How did students respond to mindful pauses?

- What personal insights did I gain as facilitator?

Encourage teachers to maintain their own mindfulness or reflective journal parallel to the students' practice.

VII. Suggested Resources

- **Primary Texts:**

    o *The Journey of Curious Philip Ajere LaBier* – Abbott, 2025.

    o *The Heart of Teaching Peace* – UNESCO Peace Education Series.

    o *Mindfulness In Plain English* - Gunaratana, 2015

    o *Being Peace* - Thich Nhat Hanh, 1996

Supplemental:

    o Audio mindfulness guides (QR links optional).

    o Local Buddhist university outreach programs (Buddhism for Education of Cambodia (BEC) and Preah Sihanouk Raja Buddhist University (PSRBU).

VIII. Closing Reflection

Peace education begins with the transformation of self.

Each lesson in this storybook is an invitation—to see clearly, think kindly, and act wisely.

When teachers embody these principles, classrooms become communities of compassion and discovery.

——— ◆ ———